For Jana Novotny Hunter

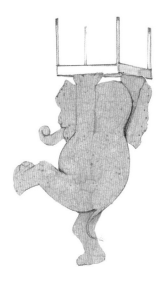

408563

When An Elephant Comes to School copyright © Frances Lincoln Limited 2004
Text and Illustrations copyright © Jan Ormerod 2004

The Publishers would like to thank Hannah Shone, aged 10, for the beautiful hand-lettering in this book.

First published in Great Britain in 2004 by
Frances Lincoln Children's Books, 4 Torriano Mews,
Torriano Avenue, London NW5 2RZ

www.franceslincoln.com

British Library Cataloguing in Publication Data available on request

ISBN 1-84507-065-8

Printed in Singapore

1 3 5 7 9 8 6 4 2

When an Elephant Comes to School

Jan Ormerod

FRANCES LINCOLN CHILDREN'S BOOKS

When an elephant
comes to school…

he may be a bit shy at first. A special friend can show him where to put his lunch-box.

Show ☆ him the toilets right away.

Making Friends

Friends are very important
to an elephant.

He likes a chat.

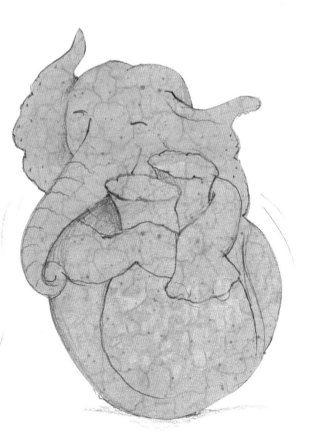

He loves to play.

An elephant wants
to join in everything.

An elephant
needs lots
of love
and cuddles
and hugs.
☆

Messy Moments

An elephant loves...

paint,

A plastic apron is a good idea. ☆

water,

glue,

and sand.

Keep a dustpan and brush near the Sandtray.

Carrying

An elephant loves to carry things...

Hold on tight! ☆

especially his friends.

How and Why?

An elephant loves to experiment.

Whoops!

An elephant can be a bit clumsy...

and elephants
are not very brave.

When he falls
over, make
a big fuss
of him.
☆

An elephant loves to eat.

Best of all he likes cake,
bananas and lemonade.

Take
an extra
sandwich.
☆

Playtime

Elephants are good at
doing tricks with a ball.

Don't let
an elephant
step on
your toes.
☆

But…

elephants are NOT
good at sharing.

If he gets cross,
he is probably
tired and thirsty.

An elephant needs
lots and lots of rest.

A quiet time with a book and a sensible friend is a good idea.

He likes stories about other elephants. ☆

TRA·LA·LA

An elephant loves music.
He likes to dance…

and march.

An elephant loves to play a tambourine. ☆

Storytime

An elephant loves a funny story…

Have a
big box
of tissues
ready.
☆

but a sad story makes him cry.

He likes to make up
his own stories.

Bye-Bye

When an elephant comes to school
he loves to make friends and have fun
learning things.

And he loves to see his mummy
at the end of the day.

"See you tomorrow, Elephant!"